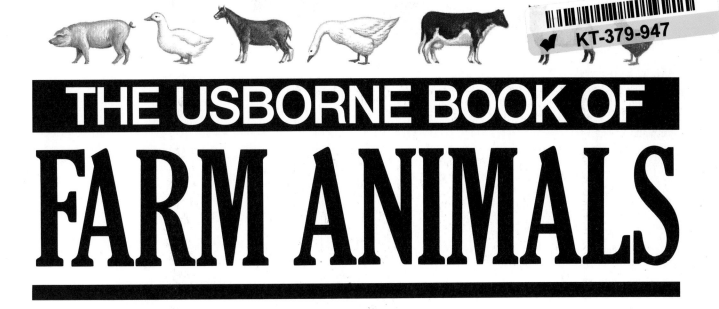

THE USBORNE BOOK OF
FARM ANIMALS

Felicity Everett

Designed by Steve Page

Illustrated by Rachel Lockwood and Myke Taylor

Consultants: Dr. Murray Black (British Society of Animal Production) and Dr. Neil Stickland (Royal Veterinary College)

Contents

Additional designs by Linda Penny
Additional illustrations by Philip Hood and Jacqueline Kearsley

About farm animals

People have kept animals for thousands of years for their meat, skins, milk, eggs and wool. In modern times, there have been big changes in the way animals are kept, but the animals themselves have not changed all that much. This book shows you each different farm animal in turn and tells you how they live, feed and care for their young.

Male and female

When you get to know the animals, it is quite easy to tell a boy animal (male) from a girl animal (female). Here you can see how a bull is different from a cow.

Cows are smaller and less chunky than bulls.

A cow has an udder for milk, but a bull hasn't.

Cows are usually gentle.

Udder

Having babies

To have babies, a male and female animal get together and mate. This is when a special liquid from the male, called sperm, goes into the female and meets a tiny, soft egg. From this moment, a baby starts to grow inside the female's tummy.

After weeks of growing in its mother's tummy, the baby is born.

Its first food is milk, which it drinks from its mother's udder.

Different breeds

Among each group of animals, such as cattle, there are different types, called breeds. The cattle shown here are from a breed called Hereford.

Bulls are large and broad, with big, strong chests. They can be quite fierce.

Different breeds vary a lot in size.

The Clydesdale and the Shetland pony are both breeds of horse.

Clydesdale horse

Shetland pony

Some breeds have very unusual markings.

These pigs are always pale pink with a few large spots on their backs. They are called Gloucester Old Spots.

Farm birds

Chickens, ducks, geese and turkeys are quite different from the other animals on the farm.

The main difference is in the way they have their young. Instead of the female growing a baby in her tummy, she lays her eggs outside and sits on them until the babies hatch.

3

Ile de France

Wensleydale

Merino

Jacob

Suffolk

Scottish Blackface

Sheep

Sheep like to live in groups called flocks. They always stay close together and follow each other around. This sometimes makes them seem a bit foolish.

Sheep that live in fields are called lowland sheep. Those that live on high ground are called hill sheep.

These are Southdown sheep. This is a lowland breed.

Sheep tear at the grass because their teeth are not very good at biting.

Farmers can tell how old a sheep is by the number of teeth it has. It gets two each year for four years.

Breeds

There are many different breeds of sheep. You can see some of them in the little pictures down the side of the page.

4

A sheep's tail is cut when it is a few days old. This is called docking.

Docking doesn't hurt the sheep. It is done because a long tail can attract germs and make the sheep ill.

This thick coat of wool is called a fleece. It keeps the sheep warm in winter.

Lowland sheep have short legs and plump bodies because they have plenty of grass to eat and don't move around much.

Hill sheep need to climb to find their food, so they are thinner than lowland sheep and have longer legs.

Wool from sheep

In early summer the sheep's fleece is cut off with electric clippers. This is called shearing. It doesn't hurt the sheep.

1. The wool is sorted out. Some is very good. Other parts are poorer.

2. It is washed. This is called scouring.

3. The wool is untangled and the long and short pieces split up.

4. The wool may then be dyed in bright shades. Not all wool is dyed. Some is left plain.

5. Then the wool is spun into yarn for knitting; or spun, then woven, into cloth.

5

Sheep farming

Sheep live outside most of the time. They don't mind the cold, but farmers do have to protect them from illness and bad weather. They may also be attacked by wild animals, such as foxes, and in some countries, wolves.

Having lambs

Ram   **Ewe**

A father sheep is called a ram. A mother sheep is called a ewe. To make lambs they mate.

A pregnant ewe

Then the ewe is pregnant. This means she has lambs growing inside her.

A lamb being born

After five months, the ewes are put in indoor lambing pens to have their babies.

This spot of blue dye shows which flock the lamb belongs to.

These two lambs were born together of the same mother. Some ewes have three babies, and others only one.

Young lambs are very playful. They run and skip around.

Suckling

A newborn lamb gets to its feet quickly and begins to suck milk from its mother's udder. This is called suckling. Milk is the only food a lamb needs for 14 weeks.

An ear tag shows which ewe this lamb belongs to. The ewe wears a matching tag.

Controlling sheep

The person who looks after the sheep on a farm is called a shepherd.

The shepherd controls his flock using sheep dogs. He trains them to guide the sheep.

The shepherd calls or whistles orders to the dogs.

The dogs circle the sheep to keep them in a group.

These dogs are guiding the sheep into a pen.

Dipping sheep

Once a year, sheep are dipped in a special liquid which keeps their fleeces free of germs.

To make sure every part of the sheep is protected, the dipper ducks each one under the sheep dip for a moment.

These lambs are a few weeks old. They have been put out to graze for the first time. Now they will taste their first grass.

Cows

Cows are nosy animals, but they are also quite timid. If you go into a field of cows, they may come over to get a closer look at you, but they will soon be scared off if you speak loudly or move suddenly.

Cows can be farmed for their milk or their meat. These are dairy cows, kept for milking. You can find out what happens to their milk on pages 10 and 11.

Dairy cows often have numbers marked on their backs. This helps the farmer tell one from another when they go to be milked.

Charolais

Highland

Texas Longhorn

These are Holstein cows. They always have black and white markings, like this. Holsteins are a North American breed.

Gir

They are eating hay. This is their winter food, along with cattle cake and pickled grass (silage). In summer they eat grass.

Hereford

Breeds

There are many breeds of cow. These little pictures show how different breeds can be from one another.

Cows drink lots of water - about 60 litres (13 gallons) every day.

Cows' feet are called hooves. They are split into two large, horned toes.

Simmental

Cows around the world

In some countries farmers use cows instead of machines to help them work the land because they cost less.

Milk is an important food everywhere. In some countries a farmer may keep just one cow which is milked by hand to provide for the needs of the family.

In India, people of the Hindu religion believe that cows are very special and should not be harmed. If one lies down in the road, the traffic waits for it.

Cows always seem to be "chewing the cud". This means that they bring food back up after they have swallowed it and chew it again.

The cow uses her tail to swish away flies.

The udder is where the cow's milk is made and stored.

The milk is either sucked out by her calf, or by a milking machine on the farm.

Calves and milking

A cow cannot make milk until she has had a calf. When the calf starts to suck its mother's udder, the first milk comes.

Having calves

A cow and bull make a calf by mating.

A pregnant cow

Then the cow is pregnant. The calf grows inside her for about nine months.

A newborn calf soon learns to stand up and feed.

At last the calf is born. Its mother sniffs and licks it all over to get to know it.

Milking cows

When the calf has been weaned (see below), the cow still makes milk. Now the farmer can take it to sell.

This calf is sucking milk from its mother's udder through a teat.

The first milk that comes is called colostrum. It is full of goodness and helps keep the calf healthy.

Teat

Milking shed

1. Cows are milked twice a day, in the morning and evening.

2. Each cow passes through a stall in the milking shed.

3. Special sucking hoses are slipped onto her teats.

4. When the milking machine is switched on, the milk is sucked through the tubes into these measuring bottles.

5. This big tank collects the milk from the cows and keeps it cool and clean.

The cow rubs her calf's body gently with her nose, while he drinks. This is called nuzzling.

6. A tanker comes to take the milk to a dairy, where they prepare it.

7. At the dairy the milk is heated, to kill any germs, then cooled.

Weaning

At three days old, the calf is taken away from its mother and fed on milk replacer. This is called weaning. Soon it will eat solid food and drink water.

8. Then it is put into bottles or cartons and sold to the people who sell it to you.

These foods all have milk in.

Chocolate

Butter

Cheese

Yogurt

Pigs

People often think pigs are dirty, stupid animals but they are neither. They can learn more quickly than horses or dogs and are naturally very clean.

Duroc

Hampshire

Large white

Gloucester Old Spot

Wild boar

Wart hog

Vietnamese pot-bellied pig

This light frightens off foxes, which might attack at night.

These are Landrace pigs. This breed is farmed in many countries, because it makes good meat.

These pigs are fully grown. They are huge and heavy - some weigh three times as much as a man.

This pig is wallowing in the mud to keep cool. Pigs do this because they cannot sweat.

These rings are to stop the pig from digging up the earth with its snout to look for food.

Pigs' feet divide in the middle to make two horned toes. Pigs' feet are called trotters.

Pig food is mainly made from ground beans, fishmeal and grain.

Breeds

The first four pigs shown in the little pictures are the kind you find on farms. Below them are three wild pigs. Pigs like these still roam free in some countries.

Keeping pigs

Some pigs live in fields and sleep in shelters called arks. They have a lot of freedom, but there are dangers too.

Pigs used to be kept in sties in the farmyard. These are stone or wooden huts with pens around them.

These days most pigs are kept indoors in pens like these. They are warm and well-fed, but they can hardly move.

The curlier a pig's tail, the healthier it is supposed to be.

A numbered ear tag helps the farmer to tell one pig from another.

13

Piglets

Mother pigs are not so good at raising their young as some other farm animals. The farmer has to keep an eye on them to make sure they feed their piglets properly and do not harm them by accident.

Having piglets

To make piglets, a sow (mother pig) and a boar (father pig) mate. The sow is then "in pig". This means she will have piglets in 16 week's time.

This sow has given birth to piglets in her nest of straw. This is called farrowing.

The newborn piglets drink milk from her udders.

A piglet is born about every 15 minutes over a few hours.

The newborn piglets have to look after themselves. The sow does not lick them clean or help them to suckle.

Farrowing crate

Each piglet returns to the same udder whenever it feeds.

Sometimes a mother pig may even squash some of her babies accidentally, by rolling over on them when they are trying to feed.

To keep them safe, the farmer may put the sow in a farrowing crate. When she lies down, the piglets creep away to the side.

14

Most sows have around ten piglets, but some have as many as 16.

By the time the piglets are three weeks old they will be eating solid food.

This weak piglet is called a runt. It has been pushed out by its brothers and sisters.

Runts often have to be bottle-fed.

Piglet play

Piglets are very playful creatures, but they sometimes harm each other by accident.

Many farmers cut their piglets' tails short to stop them from being chewed by their playmates.

To keep piglets from biting too hard when they play, the farmer may snip off the points of their teeth.

Chains or ropes may be used to hang things in the piglets' pen for them to play with.

Chickens

Chickens are quarrelsome birds. If left to themselves, males fight each other over females and females peck one another to show who's boss. Farmers keep chickens for their eggs and their meat.

Breeds

These little pictures show some of the best-known and most eye-catching breeds.

These are Rhode Island Reds - a North American breed which can also be found in many other countries.

Chickens' wings are very short, so they cannot fly far.

A chicken's beak is as strong as other animals' teeth.

Yokahama cock

Silver Campine hen

White leghorn cock

Silkie hen

Welsummer cock

Indian Game hen

The male chicken is called a cock. He is bigger and more attractive than the female which is called a hen.

Tail feathers

Comb

Wattles

Chickens scratch the ground with their sharp claws, looking for food.

Keeping hens

Free range hens roam freely outside, but sleep in a hen house at night. They eat chicken feed, insects and plants.

Perchery hens live in windowless barns, lit by electricity. The hens can move around, but the barns are very cramped.

Battery hens live in cages inside long, narrow huts. They are kept warm, clean and well fed, but can hardly move.

The cock's comb is bigger than the hen's.

The cock's bright skin and feathers attract hens to mate with him.

Most chickens are fed a mixture of cereals, fish meal, seeds and grit. They drink water.

This spur is an extra fighting claw which can be deadly to other cocks.

Turkeys

Turkeys are farmed for their meat. It tastes quite like chicken, but because turkeys are so big, there is more of it.

The male turkey is more eye-catching than the female.

This flap of skin is called a beard.

Because turkeys are bred to be very big, they often have trouble walking.

His short, curved beak is good for pecking insects and seeds.

17

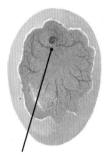

Chick's eye

Five days old

Eggs

Chickens, ducks, geese and turkeys all lay eggs to have their young. They don't grow babies in their tummies like most other animals. Eggs which have babies inside look the same as the kind you eat, but they are not.

Hens lay their eggs in nesting boxes filled with straw.

Mating and laying

To have babies, a cock and hen mate. Then the hen is fertile. The eggs she lays for the next few days will hatch into chicks. She lays about ten, then sits on them to keep them warm.

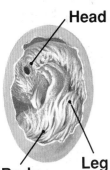

Blood vessels

Ten days old

Head

Body   **Leg**

19 days old

Inside the egg

The little pictures down the side of the page show what happens inside the eggs as they get ready to hatch.

The chick hatches.

21 days old

Newborn chicks tend to look scrawny, but their feathers soon fluff out.

Eggs and chicks

Duck egg

A baby duck is called a duckling.

Turkey's egg

A baby turkey is called a poult.

Goose egg

A baby goose is called a gosling.

The farmer's name for a hen that is sitting on her eggs is broody.

The hen's body keeps the eggs warm and slightly damp.

Every so often she turns the eggs over with her beak to warm the undersides.

She protects the eggs fiercely and will attack anyone who disturbs her.

The eggs we eat

The eggs we eat are not fertile. They cannot hatch into chicks. Most people eat eggs which come from battery hens.

Every day the eggs are collected and sorted into different sizes.

Then they are put in boxes and sold to shops and supermarkets.

You can cook and eat eggs on their own, or use them to make other dishes.

Water birds

Geese and ducks are water birds. They are farmed for their meat or eggs. They are kept outdoors near a pond or puddle.

This brightly-feathered duck is called a Rouen. It is a male, or drake. The female is smaller and plainer.

Ducks and geese swim very gracefully, but they can look clumsy waddling around on land.

Geese

This is an Embden goose. It is a German breed which is farmed for its meat.

These big wings should make ducks good fliers, but farm ducks have been bred to be heavier than wild ones, so they cannot fly far.

Geese are also useful to farmers because they crop the grass in fields and orchards.

They make very good burglar alarms too. They will hiss and honk if they are worried by a stranger.

Keeping ducks

Ducks need space as well as water to thrive. They cannot be crowded together like chickens.

By day, they live in large wire pens, or roam free. At night they sleep in huts to protect them from wild animals.

The female duck lays her eggs in a nest and sits on them for almost four weeks until they hatch.

Farmers feed ducks on grain, but they also eat grass, worms, slugs and water plants.

Ducks and geese moult in the summer. This means that some of their feathers fall out to make room for new ones. Fallen feathers can be collected and used to stuff pillows and quilts.

Oil in their feathers stops water from soaking into them.

Its spoon-shaped bill helps the duck to shovel up food and water.

Webbed feet help ducks and geese to swim easily.

21

Horses

Long ago, horses were used on farms to do the work that machines do now. They pulled along tools, or carts with heavy loads.

Why keep horses?

Cattle and sheep farmers with very large farms or ranches sometimes keep horses for visiting their animals in fields far away.

Some farmers keep very large horses called Shire horses for show. You might see Shire horses giving wagon rides at a country fair.

Some farms also have horse-riding stables. People pay for riding lessons and to go out on horseback.

These horses are Clydesdales. This breed make good work horses because they are big and strong, yet gentle.

Horses use their tails to flick flies away.

A baby horse is called a foal. Within a few minutes of its birth a foal can stand up and take its first wobbly steps.

Withers

Hock

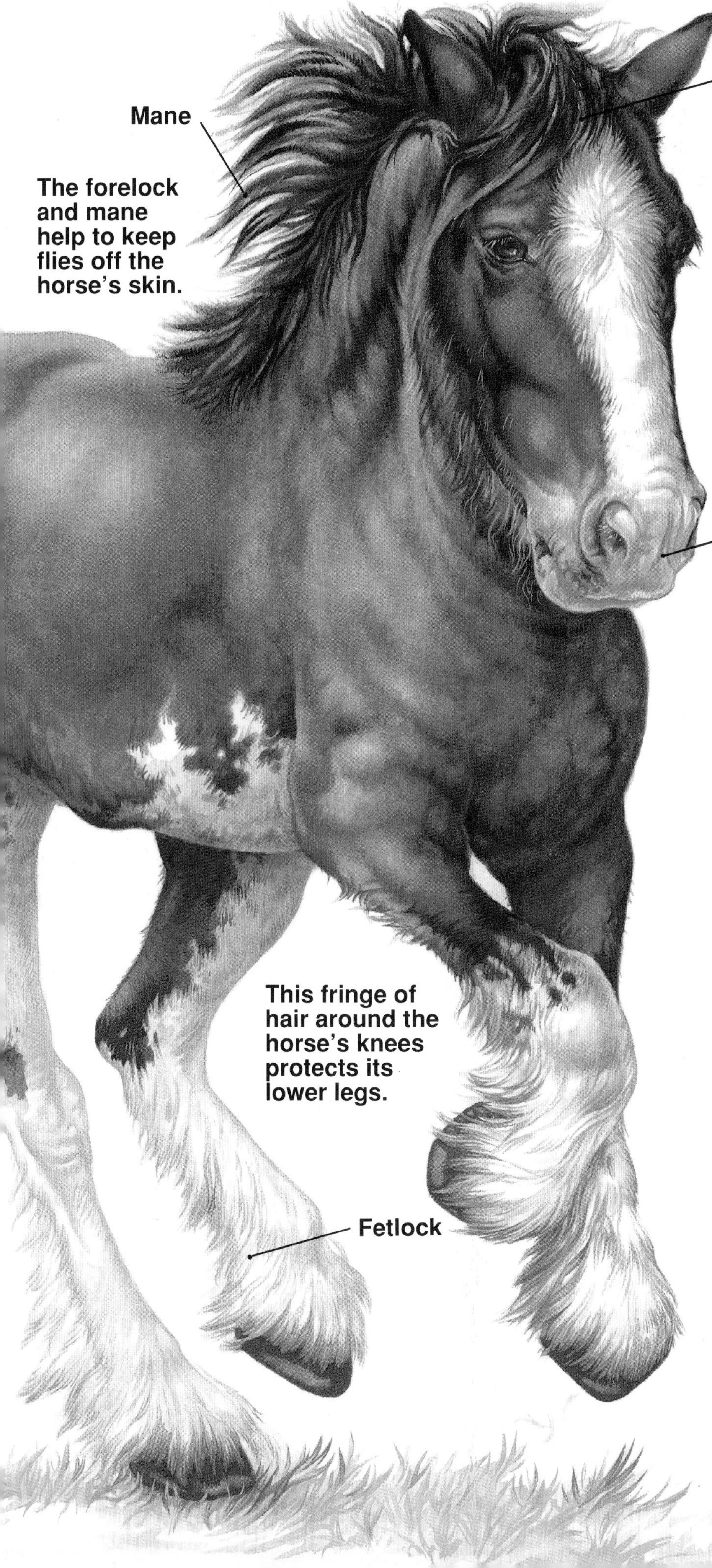

Mane

Forelock

The forelock and mane help to keep flies off the horse's skin.

Horses have very sharp ears. If they sense danger or are angry, they put their ears back.

A female horse is called a filly until she is four, then a mare.

A male horse is known as a colt until he is four, then a stallion.

Muzzle

Horses eat grass in the summer and hay in the winter.

This fringe of hair around the horse's knees protects its lower legs.

Horses are measured in hands. This used to be a rough measurement based on the width of an adult's hand. These days it is exactly 10cm (4in).

Most fully-grown Clydesdales measure between 16 and 17 hands. That's about as tall as an average adult .

Fetlock

Donkeys

Donkeys are gentle creatures, but they can also be very stubborn. They are used in many countries to carry heavy loads and pull carts. They are very strong and, once they get going, they can travel long distances over rough ground.

Farmers often keep donkeys as companions for horses, because they are calm and friendly.

Donkeys are stronger for their size than horses or ponies. This is why they are often used as working animals.

If a female horse and a male donkey mate, the baby that they make is called a mule.

Donkeys are related to horses but they are not a breed of horse.

You can sometimes ride on a donkey at a fair or at the seaside.

This soft harness stops the donkey's skin from being rubbed as it pulls the heavy cart.

Donkeys are usually grey or brown with a darker, cross-shaped pattern on their backs.

A male donkey is called a jackass, a female is known as a jenny.

Baby donkeys are called foals.

Donkeys eat grass and straw, but they will eat much rougher greenstuff, such as thistles.

They look more furry than horses because donkeys' hair is longer and softer than horses' hair.

Donkeys' hooves, though small, are strong and nimble. This helps them to cross rough ground without stumbling.

25

Goats

People often think goats are a menace because they eat anything and everything. In fact, they are curious creatures who nibble things to find out what they are. They do not always go on to eat them.

Baby goats are called kids. These kids are butting each other in fun.

Breeds

These little pictures show some of the different breeds of goat from around the world.

Anglo nubian

Bagot

Toggenburg

Angora

Saanen

Granada

African Pygmy goat

This is a female, or nanny goat.

This is a male goat. He is called a billy.

These are British Alpine goats. This breed makes lots of milk.

Hooves

Milk is made and stored in the nanny's udder.

Beneath the goat's shaggy coat is a layer of soft, downy fur called cashmere. It is good for making fluffy sweaters.

Goats are very good at climbing and balancing. Kids are very playful. They hop and skip around and nip each other.

Male and female goats can both have horns. These protect them from other animals which might attack.

Hill goats

In some countries, where there are not many grassy fields, goats are kept on bare hillsides.

Twice a day they are brought down the hill to be milked.

They cannot be rounded up, like sheep. Instead they are led by a goatherd.

Goatherd

These goats are fed on hay and cereals such as oats and barley. They also nibble grass and other plants.

The goatherd looks after the goats.

This tuft of hair is called a beard. All billy goats have them and some nannies, too.

Goats are usually milked by hand. More people in the world drink goat's milk than cow's milk.

27

Rare breeds

You can probably tell what these different kinds of farm animal are, but you may not have seen any which look quite like them. This is because they are all rare breeds. Rare means that there are not many of them around.

Why are they rare?

Farmers have always bred animals to give more of the things people needed, such as meat, milk or wool. The best breeds for farmers were the ones that gave most of these things. The others became more and more rare.

Farming rare breeds

Some farmers still keep rare breeds. They make money by opening their farms to visitors, who pay to see the animals.

Some rare breeds have been around for hundreds of years, so they are sometimes hired out to star in films about the past.

This Eriskay pony comes from a group of islands near Scotland.

This Bagot goat is a British breed which became rare because it doesn't make much milk.

Both nanny and billy Bagot goats have horns.

This funny looking animal is a Vietnamese pot-bellied pig.

They are usually kept as pets, not for their meat or skin. They are good at keeping grass short.

Eriskay ponies were needed because farmers on the islands did not use tractors or cars until long after they had taken over in mainland Scotland.

The longhorn cow is a very old breed. It looks much like the cattle seen in paintings done by cavemen thousands of years ago.

Hebridean sheep, like this one, became rare because their dark wool was hard to dye.

This is a Yokahama cock. It is a fancy breed from Japan.

These birds are bred for their beautiful looks, not for their meat or eggs.

Hebridean rams can have up to six horns.

Friends and enemies on the farm

Every farm has some uninvited guests living on and around it. Some of them are friends which help the farmer. Others are enemies which hunt farm animals or steal their food.

Some farmers build special owl doors to their barns because they like owls to nest in them.

Barn owls

Barn owls are the farmer's friends because they hunt animals such as rats and mice. These small animals destroy the farmer's crops and steal food from farm animals' troughs.

Owls can see very well in the dark.

Powerful wings help the owl to swoop down on the animal it is hunting. This is called its prey.

This owl is clutching its prey in its sharp claws as it flies back to the nest.

Other friends

Like owls, cats hunt rats and mice, so farmers are happy to have them on the farm.

Many farmers keep guard dogs such as this German Shepherd to scare off wild animals.

Foxes

The fox is the farmer's enemy because it sometimes steals small animals from the farm. Piglets, lambs and chickens all make a tasty meal for a hungry fox.

Farmers keep their animals locked up at night. They also try to scare away foxes with lights or guns.

The fox's bushy tail helps it to balance and change direction quickly.

Its sharp ears listen for sounds of danger.

The fox has a good sense of smell. It sniffs out animals to eat.

The fox moves quickly and quietly, sneaking up on its prey before it is aware of danger.

Other enemies

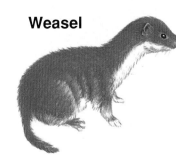

Rabbit

Weasel

Coyote

Rabbits and hares are pests because they eat crops that are meant for farm animals or people.

Weasels and stoats kill rats and mice, but they also steal eggs and chicks from the farm.

In some countries wolves and coyotes live near farms and hunt sheep and calves.

Index

First published in 1993 by Usborne Publishing Ltd, Usborne House, 83-85 Saffron Hill, London EC1N 8RT, England. Copyright © 1993 Usborne Publishing Ltd.
First published in America August 1993. The name Usborne and the device ♀ are Trade Marks of Usborne Publishing Ltd.